Praise for *Gabriel*

"*Gabriel* is a story of hope and inspiration. My own children's drive to make the world a better place is what inspires me to work every day toward a future where no animal is exploited for food. Their passion fuels mine. I look forward to a future where the world's children will look at cows, and all animals, as beautiful, smart creatures, worthy of respect, protection, and freedom."—**Leah Garcés**, President, Mercy For Animals

"*Gabriel: How Saving One Calf Changed an Entire Community* is a book I wish I was given to read as a child. Cheryl Moss has written a story that allows children to learn about the harsh realities of our food system in a gentle, but honest way. At the same time, children are empowered to follow their hearts, be courageous, and solve problems that will make this world better. The artwork by Irene Blasco enhances this truthful narrative. The colorful illustrations reveal the life in the animals' eyes—eyes that are full of feeling, be it fear, sadness, or joy. Knowing the reality of where food comes from, children will be motivated to find solutions that are kind, just, and sustainable for people, animals, and the environment."—**Caryn Hartglass**, Co-Founder and President, Responsible Eating And Living

"This is a beautiful book by Cheryl Moss, with its wonderful message to young people that they *can* make a difference. The story of *Gabriel* unfolds concisely and directly, yet at the same time draws the reader into a deeper awareness of the power of compassion and empathy. The illustrations by Irene Blasco are a perfect fit, filled with sensitivity and warm colors that enhance the impact of the book."—**Dr. Joanne Kong**, editor of *Vegan Voices: Essays by Inspiring Changemakers*

"Congratulations. This is an absolutely fantastic book that I wish all youth would read. I love this story of awakening, a bold first animal rescue by a young teenage girl, and how it brings together compassion for animals and a concern for the climate and water crises. It's poignantly illustrated in both realist and expressionist styles."
—**Anita Krajnc**, PhD

"*Gabriel* offers a glimpse of a world where love and connection to all sentient beings is the norm. An eye-opening, thought provoking, deeply moving and timely book,

Gabriel 'wakes up' and inspires young and adult readers to create positive change for all animals, the earth, and as a result, humankind."—**Camille Licate**, speaker, author, creator of Kids for Positive Change & Wake Up with Bree (the Rescue Rooster) www.WakeUpwithBree.com

"I react viscerally to artist Irene Blasco's rendering of this story of Gabriel and the other animals. One can't help but see these paintings and become immersed. Thus gripped, I wanted to see more, and *know* more. The images are beautiful, highly emotionally intelligent, and succeed in their goal: they also made me want to *do* more."—**Jo-Anne McArthur**, photojournalist, Founder of We Animals Media

"Bravo that this team came together to tell the children the truth! The honest portrayal of what animals endure at our hands and Irene's rich illustrations in *Gabriel* bring home the message that children can understand, that peace really does begin on your plate." —**Jodi Paige**, Virgin Cheese

"If you want to raise kind and compassionate children, this is the book you are looking for. With gorgeous illustrations and objective yet graceful language, *Gabriel* depicts the philosophy of veganism through a carefully constructed story on the ramifications of raising animals for food. I love how the author uses a child-friendly narrative that also inspires adults to make higher choices."—**Dr. Camila Perussello**, Food Engineer, Gaia Vida Consciente

"Annika, our 9-year-old, and I fell in love with Gabriel's touching story. These issues impact everyone on the planet and, now more than ever, we need to open up our kids' eyes and hearts to what is going on in a compassionate way. That is exactly what this book does."—**Mikael Roldsgaard**, Director of Leadership Giving, Mercy For Animals

"There has never been more of a need for books like *Gabriel*. With Irene Blasco's vibrant illustrations, Cheryl Moss's narrative comes alive as we follow the ripple of change created by Claire, a young girl who performs one courageous and compassionate act. Young readers who hold this book in their hands will recognize in themselves the innate compassion that Claire embodies, for she demonstrates how caring about the well-being of other animals is truly an instinctual response. By describing a systemic transition away from the consumption of animal products, and the exploitation of animals becoming something of the past, *Gabriel* helps bring us closer to making this a reality."—**Linnea Ryshke**, visual artist and author of *Kindling*

GABRIEL

How Saving One Calf Changed an Entire Community

A story by Cheryl Moss

Illustrated by Irene Blasco

Lantern Publishing & Media • Brooklyn, NY

2021
Lantern Publishing & Media
128 Second Place
Brooklyn, NY 11231
www.lanternpm.org

Printed in the United States of America

Library of Congress Cataloging-in-Publication Data

Names: Moss, Cheryl, author. | Blasco, Irene, illustrator.
Title: Gabriel / a story by Cheryl Moss ; illustrated by Irene Blasco.
Description: Brooklyn, NY : Lantern Publishing & Media, [2021]
Identifiers: LCCN 2021027587 (print) | LCCN 2021027588 (ebook) | ISBN 9781590566725
   (hardback) | ISBN 9781590566732 (epub)
Subjects: CYAC: Animal rescue—Fiction.
Classification: LCC PZ7.1.M6775 Gab 2021 (print) | LCC PZ7.1.M6775 (ebook) | DDC [E]—dc23
LC record available at https://lccn.loc.gov/2021027587
LC ebook record available at https://lccn.loc.gov/2021027588

The mission of the **Better Life for Animals** website is to educate and enlighten children and people of all ages using compassionate and child-friendly content regarding the inhumane treatment of animals. While our message applies to all beings, the emphasis is on farmed animals trapped inside the business known as factory farming. The **Better Life for Animals** website accompanies a trilogy of children's books authored by Cheryl Moss published annually starting in the fall of 2021 by Lantern Publishing & Media. You can use the QR code above to access the website. All proceeds are dedicated to non-profit organizations devoted to animal rights and education. Thank you for caring about the animals and our planet.

Foreword

Caryn Hartglass
Co-Founder and President, Responsible Eating And Living

When I was a child, I was given many books to read about farms. There were toys to play with too, with farmed animals—the cows that mooed, the chickens that clucked, the pigs that oinked. Children's television cartoons were filled with talking animals. Farmed animals especially seemed to lead an idyllic life, often grazing in the pasture, and lazily resting in the sun or under a tree.

Like many children, I enjoyed hamburgers, turkey on Thanksgiving, ice cream, and cheese omelets.

It wasn't until I was 15 that I realized who was on my plate. My understanding of where meat, milk, and eggs came from was based on lies. The realization stunned me, and I couldn't understand how everyone thought it was normal to kill animals in order to eat their flesh. I was told we needed to eat meat for protein. It made us strong. Even the family physician told me it was good to eat meat because more cows were given the opportunity to live. Intuitively, this did not make sense, and I started on a path that led me to adopt a vegan lifestyle.

Many decades later, I know that farmed animals live miserable lives. We don't need to eat animals to be healthy—quite the contrary, the science shows that humans thrive on a plant-based diet and have greater risk of chronic disease the more animal foods they consume. Raising animals to feed people is inefficient. It wastes resources while causing environmental degradation.

Gabriel: How Saving One Calf Changed an Entire Community is a book I wish I was given to read as a child. Cheryl Moss has written a story that allows children to learn about the harsh realities of our food system in a gentle, but honest way. At the same time, children are empowered to follow their hearts, be courageous, and solve problems that will make this world better. Knowing the reality of where food comes from, children will be motivated to find solutions that are kind, just, and sustainable for people, animals, and the environment.

The artwork by Irene Blasco enhances this truthful narrative. The colorful illustrations reveal the life in the animals' eyes—eyes that are full of feeling, be it fear, sadness, or joy. It is easy to see in these stunning pictures how cows and pigs are more like us than not, deserving of our love, care, and respect as much as our family dogs and cats.

Children deserve age-appropriate honesty about where food comes from, not a sugar-coated version. *Gabriel: How Saving One Calf Changed an Entire Community* is a wonderful, compassionate book to begin teaching children the truth.

Claire grew up at a time when dogs were pets that families would love and care about. Same with cats.

But it was also a time when other animals who were just as smart and just as adorable were raised to become meat on Claire's plate. These animals were not offered the love and comfort so many pets were given.

It only worked on the surface because people had learned to turn off their feelings for other animals.

They convinced themselves that they needed this meat to survive, and that, therefore, it was their right.

But underneath, most people knew the animals were suffering.

And increasingly, this was making people sick with disease.

This was a time when animals and humans were strangers to each other.

Farm cows, pigs, and chickens were nameless, faceless creatures.

They wore tags like tattoos. They grew up tightly packed with other animals known as livestock without regard for their health or comfort.

Their mothers were removed from them and so they were alone in a crowd.

The land they stood on was soiled and the air they breathed hurt their lungs.

Mother Nature had built a planet where every animal had her place and her purpose. But over time, humans decided they had a right to store animals for food.

The land used to hold animals took over space that was meant to be for the trees.

The water intended to feed plants was pumped out of the soil.

Animals were moved and packed into cages. Many of them couldn't survive.

The others grew scared and sick.

It was a period of darkness. The skies were gray, the waters were murky, and the planet was growing hotter by the day.

So, Mother Nature put humankind on notice. This time, she sent a coronavirus sickness that connected humans to those same mistreated animals. She sent a sickness through the air that forced humans to stay home and only venture out when wearing a mask.

People who were forced to work closely together got sick.

This interrupted people's plans. It made taking animals and turning them into food dangerous for humans.

Claire was there the day the food processing plants were shut down due to illness. This meant all of the animals ready to be transported to their death had nowhere to go. Farmers were traumatized.

Claire saw a line of cows and another of pigs whose fate appeared to be doomed.

Claire looked closer. She could see their faces.

Their tag numbers transformed into names. These beautiful creatures were terrified.

They missed love and connection, which had been taken from them when they were young. Claire could hear their cries for the first time and felt a deep sadness.

Claire felt so helpless in the face of this enormous tragedy.

But she saw them. No one could tell her that she was too young to know what was really happening here.

Telling her that this is how this has always been done didn't make anything about it right.

There was a cage with a baby calf locked inside.

He was all alone, shaking in a pen so small he couldn't move. All of the other cages were empty, but somehow this little calf was overlooked.

Claire looked closer. He had a tag on his ear. It read, "VEAL3T3".

But once they looked into his eyes and saw what Claire had known all along, they settled down.

Claire exclaimed, "I'm naming him Gabriel."

Gabriel received love and kindness, and gave back the same.

He was such a sweet and gentle soul. Claire was amazed at how smart he was.

Gabriel remembered every face! Whenever Claire showed him a photo of another cow, Gabriel would light up.

She saw how Gabriel loved the days when the sun was out, but hated the rain.

She saw how Gabriel loved the days when the sun was out, but hated the rain.

Once the community caught wind of the story of the little girl who saved Gabriel from certain death, more people stepped in to defend her decision. It was true, after all, that animals were suffering needlessly whenever humans ate their meat or drank their milk.

Humans didn't need this to thrive.

They were drinking milk that belonged to the babies of cows, sheep, and goats.

It wasn't good for anyone. This same milk that couldn't get sold because of the human sickness, was poured down the drain.

What a waste of food, and even worse, what a loss for those grieving cows and all of their motherless calves!

Whenever Claire fed Gabriel cows' milk, his cries would change from, "Moo" to "Mom." This surprised Claire as well as her family.

Claire talked about Gabriel whenever she could, even on video calls. He became beloved by the entire community.

His cry of "Mom" went viral.

Billboards sprung up across the country.

His presence reminded people of all of the suffering livestock were put through, and it prompted many to make kinder, healthier choices.

People started eating more fruits and vegetables grown near their local markets.

Gabriel would eat the grass that had been growing since the humans, hiding from the virus, had been sent indoors.

Gabriel would drink the clean water and breathe the clean air.

With humans taking a break, the planet was able to heal, and people had a decision to make. Live off of fruits, grains, and vegetables Mother Nature provides all of her children, and see the beauty and humanity in all.

Or go back to "normal," until the next time...

But Claire would never be going back.

She was awake now and forever changed. With Gabriel at her side, Claire was able to help many make better choices.

Because when we know better, we have an opportunity to do better.

How about you?

Epilogue

Leah Garcés, President, Mercy For Animals

In the year 2050, the children who read this book will live in a very different world. By then, today's youngest generations may have lived through even more pandemics—as unimaginable as that seems to us right now. They will have witnessed the extinction of many more species, watched more rivers run dry, and watched forests burn to make way for pastureland. Given humanity's current course, the world of the future could look very dark.

But I believe it will be bright. I have hope that we and our children, inspired by young people's inherent love for animals and our planet, will have turned down a better path. Young activists like Claire will show us the way, leading with compassion and bravery. My own children's drive to make the world a better place is what motivates me to work every day toward a future where no animal is exploited for food. Their passion fuels my own.

By 2050, I believe healthy, plant-based food will be more accessible to all. Animals will no longer end up on restaurant menus, which instead will feature delicious meals made of fresh vegetables, grains, mushrooms, beans, and fruits. These crops will flourish on land formerly used to raise animals. Farmers will sleep easy at night knowing they're feeding the world with foods that nourish both people and the planet. Communities will be healthier and happier. Wildlife will thrive in harmony with humans. Earth will be cooler, cleaner, and greener.

It is an honor to create this world through my work at Mercy For Animals, an international organization devoted to ending industrial animal agriculture and creating a better food system. We fight for companies to treat animals better, help governments pass laws to protect animals, and inspire thousands to join us to drive change.

Together, I know we can build a better future for animals. It is up to us.

And if we succeed, by 2050, all the world's children will look at cows (and other animals!) just like Claire looks at Gabriel—as beautiful, smart creatures worthy of respect, protection, and freedom.

To learn more and join us, please visit mercyforanimals.org.

The mission of the **Better Life for Animals** website is to educate and enlighten children and people of all ages using compassionate and child-friendly content regarding the inhumane treatment of animals. While our message applies to all beings, the emphasis is on farmed animals trapped inside the business known as factory farming. The **Better Life for Animals** website accompanies a trilogy of children's books authored by Cheryl Moss published annually starting in the fall of 2021 by Lantern Publishing & Media. You can use the QR code above to access the website. All proceeds are dedicated to non-profit organizations devoted to animal rights and education. Thank you for caring about the animals and our planet.

About the Author and Illustrator

Cheryl Moss understands the unconscionable misuse and exploitation of animals and the impact on our environment and pandemics. She believes in creating a children's book series about alternative ways of thinking and living to foster fundamental change. With her husband, she created the non-profit Let's Share a Dog, whereby lonely people could be connected with busy people in their own neighborhood through the mutual love of dogs. She has written two books, *Jenny the Magical Dog Next Door* and *Jenny Saves the Day*. Cheryl is a staunch animal activist and vegan who resides in Las Vegas, Nevada.

Irene Blasco is a Spanish illustrator, designer, and painter based in Valencia, Spain. Taking an intuitive approach, she primarily works with digital techniques in a versatile style that accentuates her use of color. She loves photography and since 2010 has taught art workshops for children. Her work has been recognized with prestigious awards, such as the Bologna Ragazzi Digital Award in 2013 for her interactive storybook *Rita the Lizard*. Irene is also the winner of the LIBER 2021 Illustration Award.

About Mercy For Animals

Mercy For Animals exists to end one of the greatest causes of suffering on the planet: the exploitation of animals for food, in particular, industrial animal agriculture, aquaculture, and fishing. These forms of food production cause egregious animal suffering and have detrimental effects on the planet and people. Mercy For Animals' mission is to construct a compassionate food system that is not just kind to animals, but essential for the future of our planet and all who share it. Their vision of a world where animals are respected, protected, and free drives the work we do every day.

You can learn more at mercyforanimals.org.

About the Publisher

Lantern Publishing & Media was founded in 2020 to follow and expand on the legacy of Lantern Books—a publishing company started in 1999 on the principles of living with a greater depth and commitment to the preservation of the natural world. Like its predecessor, Lantern Publishing & Media produces books on animal advocacy, veganism, religion, social justice, humane education, psychology, family therapy, and recovery. Lantern is dedicated to printing in the United States on recycled paper and saving resources in our day-to-day operations. Our titles are also available as ebooks and audiobooks.

To catch up on Lantern's publishing program, visit us at www.lanternpm.org.

facebook.com/lanternpm
instagram.com/lanternpm
twitter.com/lanternpm